Hayner Public Library District - Alton
W9-ABJ-995

OFF GO THEIR Engines. OFF GO THEIR Lights.

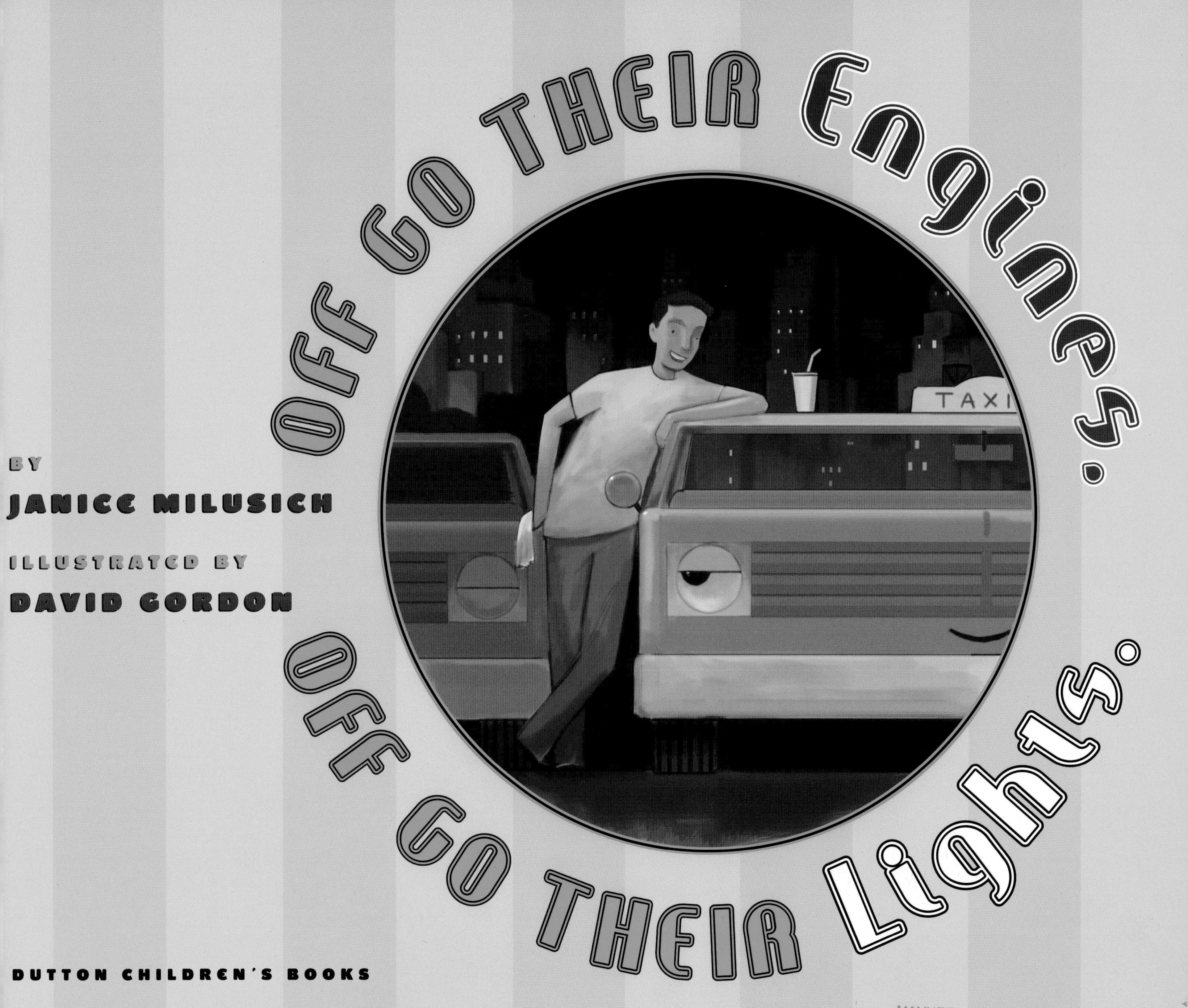

BY

JANICE MILUSICH

ILLUSTRATED BY

DAVID GORDON

DUTTON CHILDREN'S BOOKS

To Peter, whose love of cars and lack of sleep inspired this story

—J.M.

For Iola, Leif, and Oliver

—D.G.

DUTTON CHILDREN'S BOOKS | A division of Penguin Young Readers Group

PUBLISHED BY THE PENGUIN GROUP | Penguin Group (USA) Inc., 375 Hudson Street, New York, New York 10014, U.S.A. * Penguin Group (Canada), 90 Eglinton Avenue East, Suite 700, Toronto, Ontario, Canada M4P 2Y3 (a division of Pearson Penguin Canada Inc.) * Penguin Books Ltd, 80 Strand, London WC2R 0RL, England * Penguin Ireland, 25 St Stephen's Green, Dublin 2, Ireland (a division of Penguin Books Ltd) * Penguin Group (Australia), 250 Camberwell Road, Camberwell, Victoria 3124, Australia (a division of Pearson Australia Group Pty Ltd) * Penguin Books India Pvt Ltd, 11 Community Centre, Panchsheel Park, New Delhi - 110 017, India * Penguin Group (NZ), 67 Apollo Drive, Rosedale, North Shore 0632, New Zealand (a division of Pearson New Zealand Ltd) * Penguin Books (South Africa) (Pty) Ltd, 24 Sturdee Avenue, Rosebank, Johannesburg 2196, South Africa * Penguin Books Ltd, Registered Offices: 80 Strand, London WC2R 0RL, England

Library of Congress Cataloging-in-Publication Data
Milusich, Janice.
Off go their engines, off go their lights / by Janice Milusich ; illustrated by David Gordon. — 1st ed.
p. cm.
Summary: Having completed their daytime tasks, various vehicles get ready for a restful night.
ISBN 978-0-525-47940-6 [1. Night—Fiction. 2. Motor vehicles—Fiction. 3. Bedtime—Fiction.]
I. Gordon, David, date, ill. II. Title. PZ7.M6460ff 2008 [E]—dc22 2007028292

Published in the United States by Dutton Children's Books, a division of Penguin Young Readers Group,
345 Hudson Street, New York, New York 10014 * www.penguin.com/youngreaders

DESIGNED BY HEATHER WOOD
Manufactured in China * First Edition * 10 9 8 7 6 5 4 3 2 1

The setting sun warms the sky.
The buzz of the city has changed
to a hum.

**A yellow taxi cruises the avenue.
Wherever people want to go,
the taxi takes them there.**

TAXI

Always on the lookout for passengers, the taxi stops to pick up a fare and then drives through the streets as the city changes from day to night.

Lights flash, traffic stops. A red pumper truck pulls into the firehouse. A fire that flared in the corner store has been put out.

Firemen dry the truck's hoses and fill up its water tanks. If there's an emergency, the pumper will be sent out, but for now it rests.

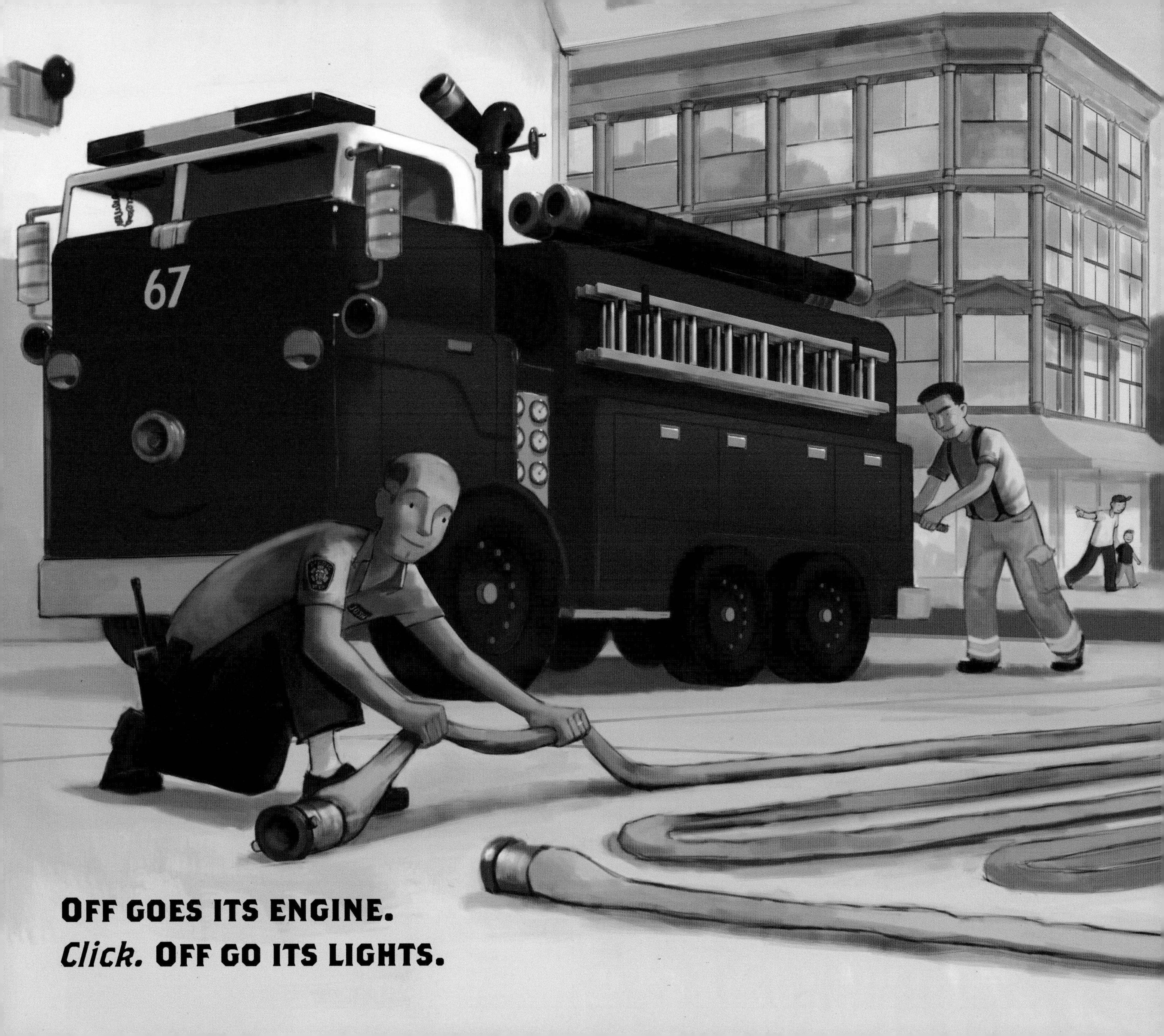

OFF GOES ITS ENGINE.
Click. **OFF GO ITS LIGHTS.**

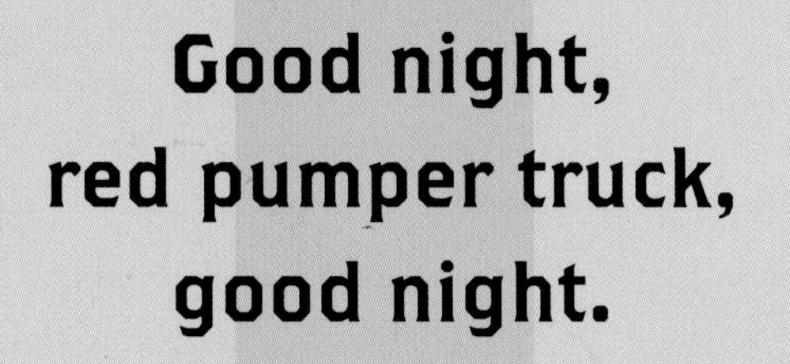

**Good night,
red pumper truck,
good night.**

The taxi waits as a green dump truck rumbles by.

All day the truck hauled dirt from a new building site. Through the open gates of the construction yard it rides.

Beep . . . beep . . . beep . . . **The tired truck backs up, spilling out its last load. Tomorrow it will move the dirt on another job, but for now its work is done.**

OFF GOES ITS ENGINE.
Click. **OFF GO ITS LIGHTS.**

Good night,
green dump truck,
good night.

Down a smooth black road
the yellow taxi drives. A
brown delivery truck rides
alongside.

All over the city, boxes of gadgets and gizmos, books and shoes were delivered today, to people in their apartment houses and shops.

Now with its hold empty, the big brown truck returns to the warehouse. There it will stay until the next day.

OFF GOES ITS ENGINE.
Click. **OFF GO ITS LIGHTS.**

Good night,
brown delivery truck,
good night.

The taxi slows as a black and white police car speeds past, sirens wailing.

One last stop to help where needed. Squad car #11 has patrolled the streets all day, making sure everyone was safe.

Now its shift is done, and another police car takes over. Outside the station, Squad car #11 is ready for a well-deserved rest.

OFF GOES ITS ENGINE.
Click. **OFF GO ITS LIGHTS.**

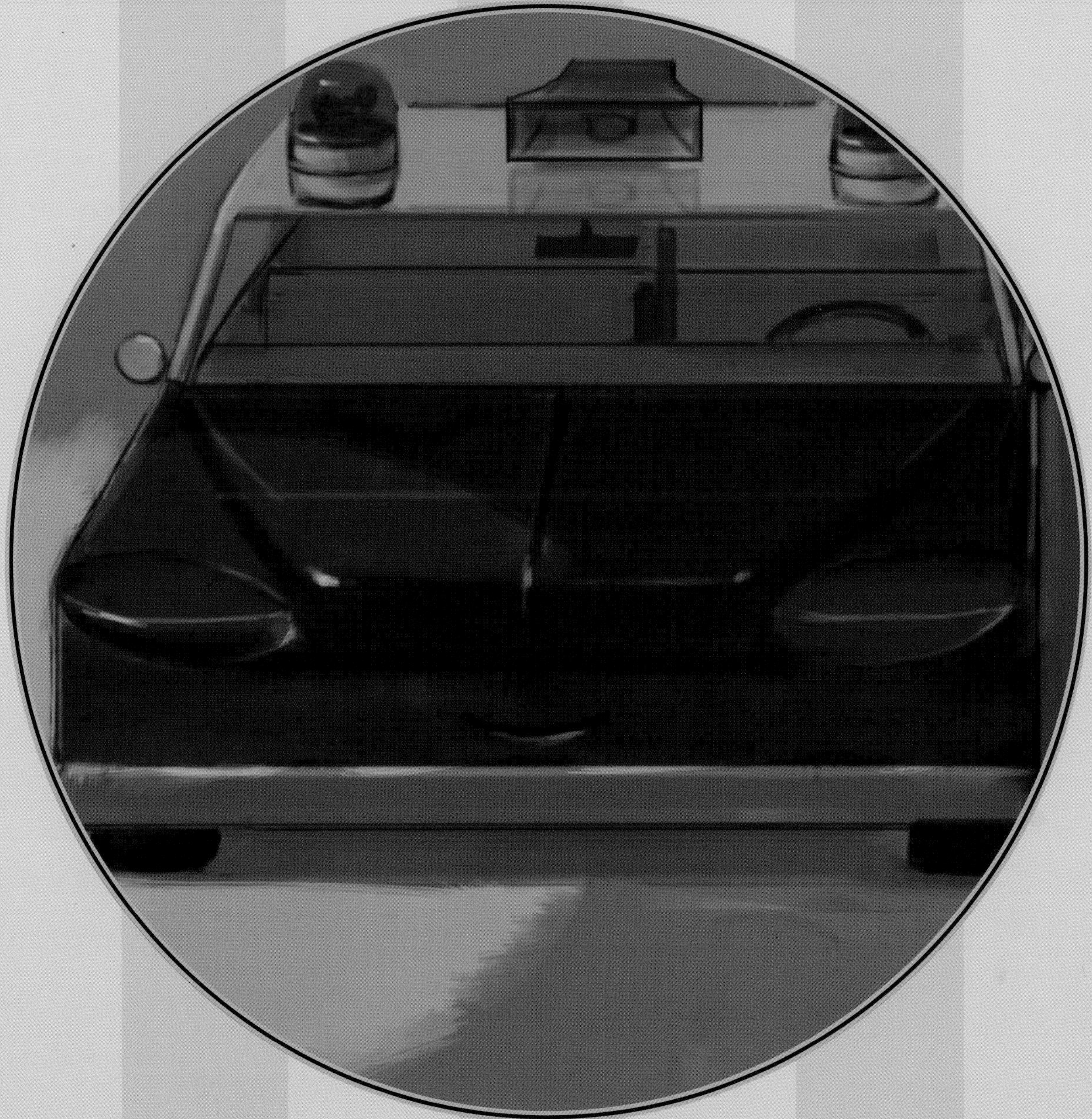

Good night,
black and white police car,
good night.

"Wait!" The yellow cab pulls up behind a blue ice-cream truck parked at the curb.

All day long the blue ice-cream truck has traveled uptown and downtown, playing its cheery music and selling icy treats.

"A vanilla and a chocolate cone, please, and a strawberry shake!"

After the last customers say good-bye, the blue ice-cream truck chugs home. Tomorrow will be another busy ice-cream day.

TAXI

OFF GOES ITS ENGINE.

Click. **OFF GO ITS LIGHTS.**

Good night, blue ice-cream truck, good night.

The taxi takes its passengers home,

and then heads back across town.

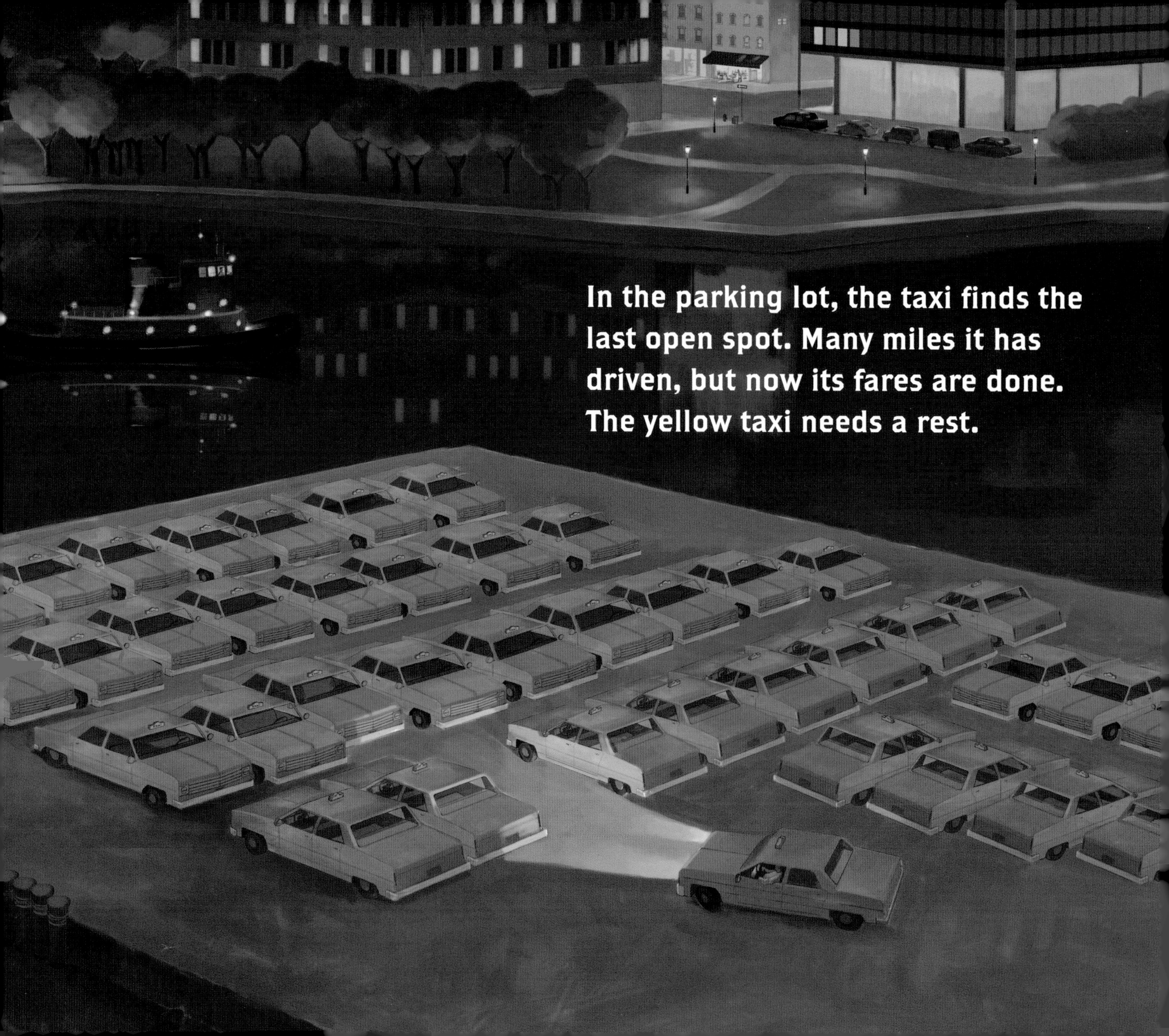

In the parking lot, the taxi finds the last open spot. Many miles it has driven, but now its fares are done. The yellow taxi needs a rest.

OFF GOES ITS ENGINE.
Click. **OFF GO ITS LIGHTS.**
Good night, yellow taxi, good night.

Tonight, the moon and stars shine bright. The cars and trucks in the city have said their good nights.

It's time now for you, little one, to turn off your engine and turn off your light.

Good night, my sweet one, good night.